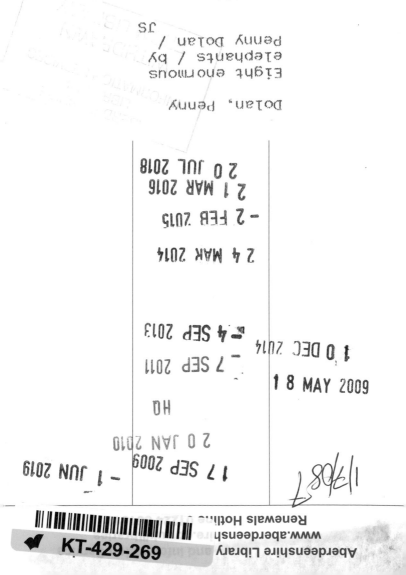

Eight Enormous Elephants

First published in 2000
Franklin Watts
96 Leonard Street
London
EC2A 4XD

Franklin Watts Australia
45-51 Huntley Street
Alexandria
NSW 2015

A CIP catalogue record for this book is available
from the British Library.

ISBN 0 7496 3926 1 (hbk)
ISBN 0 7496 4634 9 (pbk)

Series Editor: Louise John
Series Advisor: Dr Barrie Wade
Series Designer: Jason Anscomb

Printed in China

Eight Enormous Elephants

by Penny Dolan

Illustrated by Leo Broadley

W

FRANKLIN WATTS

LONDON • SYDNEY

Not just now, but a bit before ...

... eight enormous elephants came in through the door.

They squashed the sofa and they jumped on the chairs.

They danced on the table ...

and they slid down the stairs.

9

They splashed in the sink
and sploshed in the bath.

They bounced on the beds
and laughed and laughed.

They opened the cupboards
and looked in the drawers.

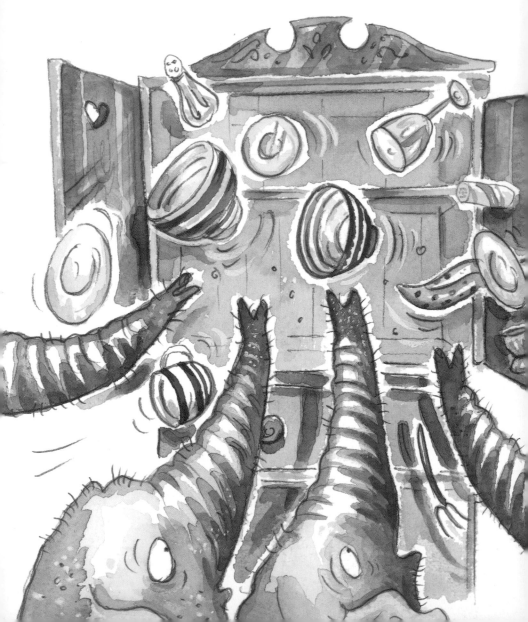

They slipped and skated
all over the floors.

I told them to go but
they said, 'No way!'
Then, all of a sudden,
a voice squeaked ...

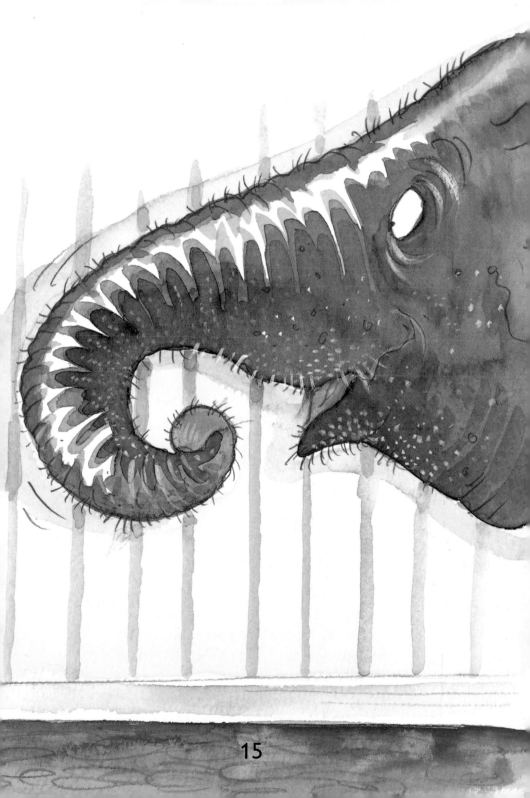

"Just sort out that sofa and straighten those chairs.

"Go wipe that table and sweep those stairs.

"Just rinse that sink and the mess that's in it.

"Go scrub that bath this very minute!

"Tidy those beds and cupboards and drawers.

"Wash those prints off all the floors!"

Then as soon as the house
was as clean as before ...

... the enormous elephants danced out of the door.

They danced away and
they left no track.

But those enormous
elephants might come back!

29

So, what do you think, Mum
What do you say?
Can I keep this mouse
that I found today?

eek!

PEPPER

30

Leapfrog has been specially designed to fit the requirements of the National Literacy Strategy. It offers real books for beginning readers by top authors and illustrators.

There are 25 Leapfrog stories to choose from: